Anonymous

Manual of Broadway Church, Chelsea, Mass.

SALZWASSER
VERLAG

Anonymous

Manual of Broadway Church, Chelsea, Mass.

Reprint of the original, first published in 1859.

1st Edition 2022 | ISBN: 978-3-37513-302-3

Verlag (Publisher): Salzwasser Verlag GmbH, Zeilweg 44, 60439 Frankfurt, Deutschland
Vertretungsberechtigt (Authorized to represent): E. Roepke, Zeilweg 44, 60439 Frankfurt, Deutschland
Druck (Print): Books on Demand GmbH, In de Tarpen 42, 22848 Norderstedt, Deutschland

MANUAL

OF

BROADWAY CHURCH,

CHELSEA, Mass.

ARTICLES OF FAITH,

AND

COVENANT;

WITH A LIST OF OFFICERS AND MEMBERS.

MARCH, 1859.

CHELSEA:
TELEGRAPH AND PIONEER PRESS.
1859.

MANUAL

OF

Broadway Church,

CHELSEA, Mass.

BROADWAY CHURCH ORGANIZED
April 2, 1851.

PRESENT OFFICERS — MARCH, 1859:

Pastor.

REV. JOSEPH A. COPP, D.D.

Installed Jan. 7, 1852.

Deacons.

IRA CHEEVER. | AZEL AMES.

Scribe.

JOSEPH H. SANDFORD.

Examining Committee.

PASTOR and DEACONS, with—
SAMUEL N. TENNY,
P. W. PRATT,
EDWARD UPHAM,
J. S. KNIGHT,
JONES VALENTINE.

FORM OF ADMISSION.

ADDRESS.

BELOVED :

You present yourselves before God and his Church, to profess your faith in the Lord Jesus Christ, and to take upon you the bonds of his Covenant. You have deeply considered the nature of this solemn transaction, and now appear in this public manner to surrender yourselves up as a living sacrifice to God through our Lord Jesus Christ.

You have been examined on your knowledge and experience of the doctrine of grace, and you will now profess your belief of the same, before these witnesses.

CONFESSION OF FAITH.

I. We believe that there is one only living and true God, the Father, the Son, and the Holy Ghost; a being possessed of every possible perfection, infinite in power, wisdom, holiness, justice, goodness, and truth.

II. We believe that the Scriptures of the Old and New Testaments are given by inspiration of God, and that they contain the only perfect rule of faith and practice.

III. We believe that God made all things for himself; and that he governs the universe according to the counsel of his own will, and that all events will be made subservient to his wise and benevolent designs.

1*

IV. We believe that man was created in the image of God, in a state of rectitude and holiness; that he fell from that state by transgressing the divine law; and that in consequence of the original apostacy, the heart of man in his natural state is destitute of holiness and inclined to evil; and that all men previous to regeneration are dead in trespasses and sins.

V. We believe that Christ Jesus has, by his sufferings and death, made atonement for sin, and that all who are saved are justified wholly by grace through the redemption which is in Christ.

VI. We believe that salvation is freely offered to all men, and that all men are under obligation immediately to embrace the gospel; but that such is the depravity of the human heart, that no man will come to Christ until he be renewed by the special agency of the Holy Spirit.

VII. We believe that all who embrace the gospel were from the beginning chosen unto salvation, through sanctification of the Spirit and belief of the truth; and that they will be kept by the power of God through faith unto salvation.

VIII. We believe that there will be a resurrection of the just and of the unjust, and a day of general judgment; and that the wicked will go away into punishment, and the righteous into happiness, both of which will be without end.

IX. We believe that in this world the Lord Jesus Christ has a visible church, the terms of admission to which are regeneration, baptism, and a public profession of faith in Christ; that the ordinances of baptism and the Lord's Supper are to be observed to the end of the world; that none but members of the visible church have a right to the Lord's Supper, and that such only have a right to dedicate their infant offspring in baptism..

Do you thus profess and believe?

[Baptism here administered.]

COVENANT.

Confessing that you are sinful, guilty, and dependent—that you have forsaken God your Maker, and lived under the influence of that carnal mind which is enmity against Him and His laws,—and henceforth renouncing the destructive ways of sin, and disclaiming all dependence on yourself, you do now, in the presence of God and men, solemnly choose and take the Lord Jehovah to be your God and Father—His equal and eternal Son, the Lord Jesus Christ, to be your only Saviour—the Holy Spirit to be your sanctifier, guide and comforter ; and the Scriptures of the Old and New Testa' ments to be the rule of your faith and practice.

DEDICATION.

In the same public and solemn manner you dedicate your_ self to God in the bonds of his everlasting covenant, unreserv-edly surrendering all that you have and are to his sovereign disposal—engaging, by his assistance, to live henceforth to Him, and not to yourself ; and to aim, whatever you do, to do all to His glory.

FIDELITY.

In humble dependence on Divine Grace, you bind yourself to a faithful and persevering performance of the various duties which you owe to God, to your fellow-creatures, and to your-self—to bring up your children and all committed to your care in the nurture and admonition of the Lord, and to use your influence, in every relation in life, to promote the cause and interest of the ever blessed Redeemer.

You also covenant and engage that you will diligently at-tend on all Christian ordinances, and hold communion in them with this Church,—especially in the ordinances of Bap-tism and the Lord's Supper ; that you will watch over the

8

Brethren in love, faithfully reproving them when they go astray ; and that you will submit to the discipline of CHRIST in his house, and to the regular administration of it in this Church—in all things seeking its peace and welfare, until re_ moved by death or regular dismission.

Do you, by the help of Divine Grace, thus profess, promise, and covenant ?

RECEPTION.

Then, in the presence of GOD and these witnesses, and in the name of our Lord Jesus Christ, you are received into his visible Church; and we, the members of this Church, [here the members of the Church rise] covenant and engage to walk towards you in the fellowship of the gospel, to watch over you in love, to admonish you in meekness when overtaken in a fault, and to seek your edification while you continue in the communion of this Church.

9

CONCLUDING ADDRESS.

AND now, beloved in the Lord, you have come under solemn
obligations, from which you cannot escape. Wherever you
go these vows will be upon you ;—and should you have occa-
sion to change your place of residence, it will be your duty to
seek, and ours to grant, a recommendation to another
Church ; for hereafter you can NEVER withdraw from the
watch and communion of the Saints, without a breach of
Covenant. You have unalterably committed yourselves, and
henceforth you must be the servants of the Lord. Hereafter
the eyes of the world will be upon you ; and as you demean
yourselves, so will religion be honored or disgraced. If you
walk worthy of your profession, you will be a credit and a
comfort to us ; but if otherwise, you will be to us a grief of
heart and a vexation. Strive, therefore, to walk in the fear
of God. Count not that you have already attained the high
moral elevation to which you should aim, but with unfailing
perseverance PRESS on until you DO attain it. Shrink not at
the cross. Remember Him who hath gone before you, and
who reckoned not his own life dear unto himself, that he
might bring you in peace to his blessed abode. And now, be
loved, we commend you to God and to the word of his grace,
which is able to build you up, and to give you and us an in-
heritance among all them who are sanctified. Amen.

OF ECCLESIASTICAL PRINCIPLES AND CHURCH ORGANIZATION.

I. This Church is subject to the Lord Jesus Christ alone and under him possesses full powers for the regulation of its own affairs, and is amenable to no other ecclesiastical body except by its own consent, and according to established Congregational usage. In the admission, discipline, and removal of its members, it will proceed according to its own understanding of the word of God.

II. Though claiming to be independent, this Church holds itself bound to the duties of Christian charity towards all Evangelical Churches, and to respect the decisions of all regular Councils, and to seek the peace and unity of all true believers in the world.

III. The permanent Officers of this Church are the Pastor and Deacons. To the Pastor pertains the office of Moderator of all meetings of the Church and Committee, and in his absence one of the Deacons ; and in absence of the Pastor and Deacons, any other member of the Church may be called to the chair. The Deacons are to assist in the administration of the Lord's Supper, provide for the poor, and aid the Pastor in the spiritual care of the flock.

IV. None shall be admitted to the communion of the Church but such persons as are sound in doctrine, without scandal in their lives, and are walking in visible holiness and cordial subjection to the Lord Jesus Christ,

REGULATIONS.

SECTION I.

ANNUAL MEETING, ETC.

ART. 1. All meetings of the Church for business or other-wise shall be opened with prayer.

ART. II. At an annual meeting of the male members of the Church, to be held the last Monday evening in December, of each year, there shall be chosen by ballot a standing Committee, Scribe, and Treasurer.

ART. III. It shall be the duty of the Standing Committee, of which the Pastor and the Deacons shall form a part— 1. To meet from time to time as a Board of Examination of candidates for church-membership. 2. It shall be their duty to act as a Committee of Inquiry and Discipline. 3. They shall also assist the Pastor and Deacons in the visitation of the Church and Congregation, and at the annual meeting report the condition of the Church.

ART. IV. It shall be the duty of the Scribe to make and preserve a fair record of the doings of the Church and Standing Committee.

ART. V. It shall be the duty of the Treasurer to keep the funds of the Church, and all collections for charitable objects, subject to the disposition of the Church.

ART. VI. There shall be a monthly meeting of the Church for business, to be notified by the Scribe and held on the first Monday evening in each month.

ART. VII. Seven members shall constitute a quorum.

SECTION II.

OF THE QUALIFICATION AND ADMISSION OF MEMBERS.

ART. I. This Church expects that each candidate for admission give evidence of regeneration, and assent to the faith and covenant of this Church.

ART. II. Candidates are to be examined by the Pastor and the Committee of the Church, chosen for that purpose, and must stand propounded before the Church and the Congregation two weeks previous to their public admission, except in extraordinary cases ; and the question of admission must be taken by vote, in a meeting of the Church.

ART. III. This Church admits members of other regular Churches to occasional communion, on condition of their complying with the rules which this Church has adopted for the regulation of its own members; but not for a longer time than one year, unless they assign satisfactory reasons for delaying to produce dismissions and recommendations from the Churches to which they belong.

ART. IV. Members of other Churches wishing to unite with this Church are received when they produce a regular dismission and recommendation, and give satisfactory evidence of piety ; being propounded at least one week before their admission.

ART. V. The Scribe is to inform candidates from the world, and members from other Churches, of their admission, also members restored after suspension or excommunication ; and present the regulations to the former.

SECTION III.

OF RELIGIOUS SERVICES.

The following Religious Services, besides the regular Sabbath worship, are established by the Church, and it will be the duty of all the members of the Church to attend them, according to their ability :—

I. Meeting Friday evening of each week, for devotional exercises, conference, and prayer.

II. Monthly Concert of Prayer for Missions, the Sabbath evening next preceding the first Monday in each month.

III. Sabbath School Concert of Prayer, the Sabbath evening next preceding the second Monday in each month.

IV. The Communion of the Lord's Supper, the first Sabbaths of January, March, May, July, September, and November.

SECTION IV.

OF CENSURES AND EXCOMMUNICATIONS.

ART. I. This Church holds itself bound to discipline its members, for all instances of vice or immorality which come to the knowledge of the Church ; and to cut off offenders from their communion, for flagrant transgressions of the moral law, or when they impenitently persist in minor offences.

ART. II. Any member, who shall deny any of the fundamental doctrines which are embraced by this Church, and which he professed on his admission, shall be admonished ; if he persists, after the first and second admonition, he shall be rejected from the fellowship of this Church.

ART. III. Any member is competent to bring a charge before the Church, against any transgressor.

2

Art. IV. Any member who is accused before the Church, shall be duly notified of the charge ; and be entitled to a fair trial, and an opportunity for making his defence.

Art. V. The confession of an accused member, or the concurrent testimony of two credible witnesses, or circumstantial evidence deemed equivalent by the Church, shall be considered sufficient for his conviction.

Art. VI. Every vote and sentence of suspension or excommunication shall be read before the whole congregation on the Sabbath next succeeding such sentence, or before a regular meeting of the Church, at the option of the officers of the Church.

Art. VII. This Church considers it the duty of every male head of a family to maintain family prayer ; a neglect of this duty will subject its members to admonition and discipline.

SECTION V.

OF WITHDRAWING FROM THE CHURCH.

Art. I. This Church will grant dismissions and recommendations to those members who are in good standing, and who conscientiously prefer uniting with other Churches with which we are in fellowship, when they apply in a regular manner and with a Christian spirit ; the application to stand over for consideration one week.

Art. II. This Church deems it irregular for their members to withdraw from them, and to unite in communion and worship with other Churches, either on account of any offence, or for better edification, without giving notice to the Church, and requesting a dismission.

Art. III. It shall be the duty of every member of this Church, who may remove from the town to reside in any other place, to apply as soon as convenient for a dismission and recommendation to some regular Church of CHRIST, in or near the place of his residence. Should any member neglect to make such application within a year after his settlement in any other place, he shall not receive a recommendation from this Church, unless he assign a satisfactory reason for his delay, and produce a certificate from the Church to which he wishes to be recommended, that he has maintained a Christian character during his residence among them.

SECTION VI.

SABBATH SCHOOL.

ART. I. The Sabbath School shall be under the special care of the Church and its Officers.

ART. II. The officers of the School shall be a Superintendent, Assistant Superintendent. Scribe, and Librarian ; chosen annually by vote of the Teachers.

ART. III. Teachers shall be appointed by the Superintendents and Pastor ; and in case of no Pastor, the Senior Deacon shall supply his place.

ART. IV. Other arrangements necessary to the successful management of the School may be made by the Superintendents alone, or conjointly with the Teachers.

By an Order of the Church, it is hereby declared, that—
" Lightness of deportment in the sanctuary ;—
" Absence from Church on the Sabbath or Sabbath evening,

or from Church meetings (without good and substantial reasons) ;—

"Attending dancing parties, theatrical exhibitions, and playing games of chance or other games ;—and

"Attending Oratorios of Sacred Music on Sabbath evenings."—are unbecoming the members of Christ's body, and cannot be indulged in by any one without injuriously affecting the peace and prosperity of the Church.

MEMBERS.

A.

Azel Ames,   April 2, 1851. Winnisimmet Cong. Ch. Chelsea.
Louisa (Azel) Ames,   "   "   "
Mary (Chas) Adams,   "   "   "
*John G. Atkins, May 1, 1853. 3d Presbyterian Ch. St. Louis, Mo.
Susanna (W.) (Isaiah) Atkins, July 1, 1853. Cen. Cong. Ch. Boston.
Henry S. Adams, May 4 1856.
Hannah M. (Henry) Adams, May 4, 1856.
Sarah (Isaiah) Atkins, May 2, 1858.
Albert S. Austin, July 4, 1858.

B.

†Wm. C. Boon,   April 2, 1851. Winnisimmet Cong. Ch. Chelsea.
†Louisa H. (Wm. C.) Boon,"   "   "
†Elizabeth E Brown,   "   "   "
‡Benjamin Bartol,   "   "   "
Mary A. (Benj.) Bartol,   "   "   "
‡H. S. Blanchard,   }   "   "   "
 (Mrs Ed. H, Rodgers,) }
Alfred Blanchard,   "   "   "
Margaret (Alfred) Blanchard,   "   "
Julia A. (Saml.) Bassett,   "   "   "
Julia A. Bassett,   "   "   "
Celaden Bassett,   "   "   "
†Mary E. (John W.) Butts,"   "   "
Mary (Giles W.) Burrows, (W.) July 4, 1852, High-st. Ch. Lowell.
†Julia M. Boon, May 7, 1854.
†Allen F. Boon, July 2, 1854.
†Edward P. Boon, July 2, 1854.
†Clarissa Bassett (Mrs. Echlin,) July 2, 1854.
†Caroline (George) Briggs, W. Nov. 5, 1854.

2*

Alfred W. Berry, Feb. 27, 1857. Salem Church, Boston.
Alfred Blanchard, jr., May 2, 1858.
Mary A. Blanchard, May, 4, 1856.

C.

Ira Cheever,   April 2, 1851. Winnisimmet Cong. Ch. Chelsea.
M. G. (Ira) Cheever,   "   "   "
Nancy H. Cheever, (Mrs. H. Reed,)   "   "
George W. Crocker,   "   "   "
Rev. Joseph A. Copp,   Jan. 7, 1852, Pres. Ch. Sag Harbor, L.I.
Fedora F. (Jos. A.) Copp, Mar. 7, "   "   '   "
Frances Coffee,   "   "
Lucy (Edward) Chase, Aug. 31, 1855. M. E. Ch. Ashburnham, Mass.
Edward Chase, Sept. 2, 1855.
Lemuel E. Caswell,   Nov. 2, 1855. Edwards Ch. Boston.
Sophronia (Lemuel) Caswell,   "   "   "   "
Mary J. Colesworthy, Nov. 4, 1855.
†Fred'k D. Chase, May, 3, 1857.
†H. M. S. (Fred'k) Chase, May 3, 1857.
Emma H. Comer, May 3, 1857.
Eliza J. Cunningham, May 3, 1857.
Louisa R. (Tracy) Cheever, Jan. 23 1857. Cen. Ch. Fall River, Mass.
†John H Comer,   July 3, 1857. Shawmut Cong. Ch. Boston.
†Susan R (John) Comer,   "   "   "
Anna O. Cheever, Jan. 2, 1859.
Sallie (Philander) Crowell, March 6, 1859.

D.

†Simon D. Dyer,   April 2, 1851. Winnisimmet Cong. Ch. Chelsea
Charles DeBacon, March 7, 1852.   "   "
Louisa (Chas) DeBacon, Mar 7, 1852, ...
Emily DeBacon,   July 2, 1854,
Harriet A. DeBacon," 8. 1856,
Sarah DeBacon, March 6, 1859.

E.

†Francis D. Ellis,   April 2, 1851, Winnisimmet Cong. Ch. Chelsea.
†Louisa (Francis D.) Ellis, April 2, 1851,   "   "
†Sarah F. Ellis,   April 2, 1851,   "   "
†Abby W. Ellis,   " 2), "   "   "
Matilda Erving,   " 2, "   "   "
P. S. Eaton,   " 2, "   "   "
Elizabeth A. (P. S) Eaton, April 2, 1851,   ..   "
Sarah [Ellery] Eldridge,   "   "   "
Robert H. Emerson Aug. 27, 1852. Winnisimmet Con Ch. Chelsea.
*Cyrene S. [Robert] Emerson, Aug. 27, 1852."   "
Mary P. (Robert) Emerson, Jan. 4, 1855, Cong. Ch. Lawrence, Ms.
Sarah W (George) Eaton, Feb'y 27. 1857, 2d Ch. Dorchester, Ms.
Abba C. (George) Eaton, July 4, 1858.

F.

George Forsyth,   April 2, 1851, Winnisimmet Cong. Ch. Chelsea.
Rebecca B. Geo.) Forsyth, "   "   "
Chloe S. (James) Farley, Jan. 2, 1853.
Gustavus Farley, March 4, 1853, Winnisimmet Cong. Ch. Chelsea.
Amelia H. (Gustavus) Farley,   "   "
Lorena (Charles) French, May 1, 1853, 1st Cong. Ch. Bangor.
Charles R. Fisher, May 1, 1857, Salem Church, Boston.
Harriet A. Forsyth, July 2, 1854.
Janette C. Farley, January 2, 1859.
James Austin Farley,   "

G.

Elizabeth Goulding, April 2, 1851, Win Cong. Ch. Chelsea.
I. S. Gray,   "   "   "
Ann D (I. S.) Gray,   "   "   "
*Mary E. Gerrish, (Mrs. A. B. Hall,)   "   "
Susan G (David) Gould March 7, 1852,   "   "
Benjamin J. Gerrish, July 4, 1852, High Street Church, Lowell
atiida (Benj J.) Gerrish, "   "   "
James Q. Gilmore,   "
Sarah M. (J. Q.) Gilmore, "
Mark Graves,   March 4, 1853, Park Street Church, Boston.
Jennie M. Gerrish, (Mrs. Albert S. Austin,) July 2, 1854.

H.

Isaac C. Hall,   April 2, 1851, Winnisimmet Cong. Ch. Chelsea.
Susan (Isaac C.) Hall,   "   "   "
William S. Haskell,   "   "   "
Ann Hunter,   "   "   "
William B. Hatch,   "   "   "
Sarah W. (Wm. B.) Hatch,   "   "   "
*William C Hall,   "   "   "
*Emeline (Wm. C.) Hall,   "   "   "
Freeman Hinckley,   "   "   "
Mary (Freeman) Hinckley,   "   "   "
Albert B. Hull,   "   "   "
Ann D. (Micajah) Haskell, (W.)   "   "   "
†Caroline M. (Wm.) Hinckley,July 4,'52, Ch.of the Pilgrims,Boston
Eliza Haskell,   July 4, 1852, Winnisimmet Cong. Ch. Chelsea.
Frances A. Haskell,   "
Elizabeth Hanna, Dec. 31, '52, St. James' Par. Glasgow, Scotland.
Margaret Hanna, Jan. 2, 1853.
Lucia Henry, May 1, 1853.
Lucia F Henry,   "
Jane E. Haskell, July 2, 1854.
Edward E. Hoyt, March 4 1855.
David Haskell, May 1, 1857, 1st Congregational Church, Saco, Me.
Miit (David) Haskell,   "   "
Esther (Miles) Hannah, April 30, 1858, Presb. Ch. St. Andrews.

Betsey (Elisha) Holden, May 2, 1858.
Madesta W. Hatch, Jan. 2. 1859.
Anna H. Haskell, Jan. 2, 1859.

I.

†Hosea Ilsley,   April 2, 1851, Winnisimmet Cong. Ch. Chelsea.
†Abigail (Hosea) Ilsley,   "   "   "
†Ann M. Ilsley,   "   "   "

J.

†Ellen B. Johnson, (Mrs. Oakman,) Nov. 6, 1853.
Charles Johnson,   April 30, 1858, Mariner's Church, Boston.
Harriet (Charles) Johnson,   "   "   "

K.

Joshua S Knight, April 2, 1851, Winnisimmet Cong. Ch. Chelsea.
Maria H. (Joshua S) Knight,   "   "
*Henry W. Knight,   "   "
Joanna M. (Loammi) Kendall, Ap. 2), '51,   "   "
†Sarah (B. H) Knox, July 2, 1851, Tabernacle Church, Salem.
Loammi Kendall, July 4, 1852.
Rebecca (James) Knowles, Sept. 5, 1856, Trini'n Ch. Wayland, Ms.
M. E Kilburn, (W.) June 26, 1857, Cen. Ch. Fall River, Ms.

L.

Mary E. Lane,   March 7, 1852,   Presb. Ch. Sag Harbor, L. I.
†Charlotte E.Loveridge)
    (Mrs. Drew,)   } Ap. 2, 1851, Winnis. Cong. Ch. Chelaea.
†Sophia Lovell,   "   "   "
*John Lillie,   "   "   "
Eliza Ann (John) Lillie,   "   "   "
Sarah A Lillie, (Mrs. C. R. Fisher,)   "   "
Elizabeth D. Lillie,   "   "   "
Augusta, M. Lovell, April 2), 1851,   "   "
Eliza M. Lowell, July 2, 1851.
Anna M Lillie, May 6, 1855.
Stephen A Lovejoy,   Nov. 2, 1855,   Salem Church, Boston.
Jane R. (Stephen) Lovejoy,   "   "   "

M.

Salmon Miller,   April 2, 1851, Winnisimmet Cong. Ch. Chelsea.
Mary Ann [Salmon] Miller,   "   "
Lyman M.‡Miller,   "   "   "
John Murdock,   "   "   "
Priscilla (John) Murdock, "   "   "
Henry Mason,   "   "   "
†Adelaide Mason,   "   "   '
*Nancy Morrison, [W.]   "   '

†Nathaniel Matthews, Ap. 2, '51, Winnisimmet Cong. Ch, Chelsea.
†Hannah T. (Nat.) Matthews,   "   "
*Ella Matthews   "   "   "
Darius A Martin,   "   "   "
Rhoda D. (Milton) Moore, (W) Ap. 29, 1851. "   "
Ellen M. (Richard W) Merrill, July 4, 1852.
Julia C. (Henry) Mason, Nov. 7, 1852.
Estella Mason, July 2. 1851.
Julia C Mason, July 2, 1854.
‡Moses March, June 30,'54, Presb. Ch. Colchester Co. Nova Scotia.
‡Hannah (Moses) Marsh,   "   "
Martha B Morton, Sept. 5, 1856, Congregational Ch. Monson, Me.
David McLaren, July 6, 1856, Presb. Cu London, Canada West.
Hellen McCann, July 6, 1856, Winni-immet Cong. Ch. Chelsea.
Joseph S Moody, July 3, 1857, Salem Church, Boston.
Anna E. [Joseph] Moody,   "   "
William H. Matthews, Sept. 6, 1857.
Eleanor B. Mushat, March 12, 1858, Salem Church, Boston.

N.

Benj. V. Newell,   April 2, 1851, Winnisimmet Cong. Ch. Chelsea.
†Susan B. [B. V.] Newell, "   "   "
†Mary A (Warren) Newell,"   "   "
†Hervey Newell,   "   ".   "
*Martha C. (Her.) Newell,"   "   "
Harriet E. Newell,   July 2, 1854.
Sophia North,   June 30, 1851.   1st Cong. Ch. Gardner, Me.
Lois North,   "   "   "

O.

Josiah Osgood,   April 2, 1851. Winnisimmet Cong. Ch. Chelsea.
Mary A (Josiah) Osgood, "   "   "
John H. Osgood,   "   "   "
Adeline (John H) Osgood,"   "   "
‡Adeline F. Osgood,   Jan'y 2, 1853.
Edward H. Osgood,   July, 2, 1854.

P.

†J. Wentworth Pottle, April 2, 1851. Winnisimmet Cong. Ch. Chelsea.
Eunice (Nehemiah) Pratt,   "   "   "
Samuel Page,   "   "   "
Frazetta Page,   "   "   "
†John M. Prince,   "   "   "
†Eleanor C. (John M.)Prince,"   "   "
Joseph B. Prince,   "   "   "
Eliza (Jos B) Prince,   "   "   "
Herman Powers,   "   "   "
Caroline H. (Herm.) Powers,"   "   "
Phineas N. Pratt,   "   "   "
Ann Eliza (Phin. N) Pratt, "   "   "

Sophia C. (Thos G.) Philbrick, Ap. 2, '51, Win. Cong. Ch. Chelsea.
†James H Prince,   "   "   "
†Eliza F. (Jas. H) Prince,   "   "   "
Mary C. Prince,(Mrs. }
   †Chas. C Haskell,) }   "   "   "
Sophia (Pierpont) Parker, (W) Ap. 29, 1841. "   "
†Phebe B Parker, (Mrs John Buck)   "   "
Harriet N Parker,   ''   "   "
Hannah (M. M.) Piggott, March 7, 1852,   "   "
Caroline A. Powers,   Sept. 19, 1852.
Maria C. Pratt   "
Ferdinand Perschold,   Nov. 5, 1852.
Joseph L Perkins, Dec. 31, 1852. Winnisimmet Cong. Ch. Chelsea.
George H Powers, May 6, 1855.
Louisa M. (George) Patrick, Jan. 11, 1856, Win.Cong. Ch. Chelsea.
George A Patrick, May 4, 1856.
Susan G. Phipps,   July 3, 1857, Third Church, Salem, Mass.

R.

Hannah Richardson, (W.) March 4, 1853, Central Church, Boston.
Eliza H. (Eli) Russell,   March 4 1855, Park St. Church, Boston.
William Ranney,   July 8, 1856.

S.

Lydia (Isaac) Smith, April 2, 1852,Winnisimmet Cong.Ch.Chelsea.
*Elisha Sherman,   "   "   "
Mary C (Elisha) Sherman, (W)   "   "
†William H. Smith,   "   "   "
Elizabeth A. (Wm, H.) Smith,   "   "
Joseph H Sandford,   "   "   "
Mary J V. (Joseph H.) Sandford,   "   "
†Wingate P. Sargent,   "   "   "
‡Stephen Sibley,   "   "   "
‡Anne E. (Stephen) Sibley, "   "   "
James Q. A. Smith, July 2 1854.
Mary B. Snow, (Mrs.
  Jos. L. Perkins,) } Nov. 5. 1851, 1st Cong. Ch. Brewster, Ms.
Mary R. (J. Q A.) Smith, June 30,'54, 1st Cong. Ch. Dover, N. H.
Sarah M. Shannon, (Mrs. W. H. Mathews,) July 2, 1851.
Hiram Sands,   Nov. 3, 1854, First Church, Cambridge,Mass.
Sarah S. (Hiram) Sands,   "   "   "
†Mary Shean,   March 2, 1855, Free Church, Scotland.
Mira A Stevens,   June 30, 1856, 1st Ch. Mittineague, Mass.
John Stiles,   May 2, 1858, Winnisimmet Cong. Ch. Chelsea.
Sarah (John) Stiles,   "   "   "

T.

†Mary Taylor,   April 2, 1851, Winnisimmet Cong. Ch. Chelsea.
Samuel N. Tenney,   Nov. 3, 1854, Salem Church, Boston.

Sarah J. (Samuel) Tenney, Nov. 3, 1854, Salem Church, Boston.
Alonzo C. Tenney,   "   "   "
Mary E. Tenney, (Mrs. A. W. Berry.)   "   "
*Mary S. (James) Tenney, April 30, 1858, Cong. Ch. Byfield, Mass.
James O. Tenney,   May 2, 1858.   -
Elizabeth C. (Alonzo) Tenney, Jan. 2, 1859, Salem Church, Boston.

U.

Edward Upham,   June 30, 1854, Winthrop Ch. Charlestown, Ms.
L. S. (Edward) Upham,
Edward Upham, Jr. May 4, 1856.

V.

Maria V. Valentine,   July 2, 1854.
Jones Valentine,   Jan. 5, 1855, 1st Cong. Ch. Oldtown, Me.
Elizabeth J. (Jones) Valentine, "   "   "

W.

†Charles White,   April 2, 1851, Winnisimmet Cong. Ch. Chelsea.
Charles White, Jr.,   "   "   "
*Asa Webb,   "   "   "
†Susan (Ann) Webb, [W.] "   "   "
Abigail W. Woodman, [W.]   "   "
Ezekiel Woodman,   Mar. 5, 1852, First Ch. Charlestown, Mass.
Sarah Ann [Ez] Woodman, "   "   "
Sarah [David] Wyman, [W.] "   "   "
Terza [Horace] Watson,   Dec. 31, 1852, Cong. Ch. Dorchester, Ms.
Mary E White,   Jan. 2, 1853.
Jere. W. Walker,   July 2, 1854.
†Louisa W. [Samuel] Walker. Nov. 5, 1854.
†Louisa W. Walker, May 6, 1855.
Clara Ann [Thomas] Whittemore, July 1, 1855.

Members received by letters,	194
do. do. profession,	68
	—— 262
Members deceased,	13
do. dismissed to other churches,	47
do. excommunicated,	7
Present number of members,	195
	—— 262